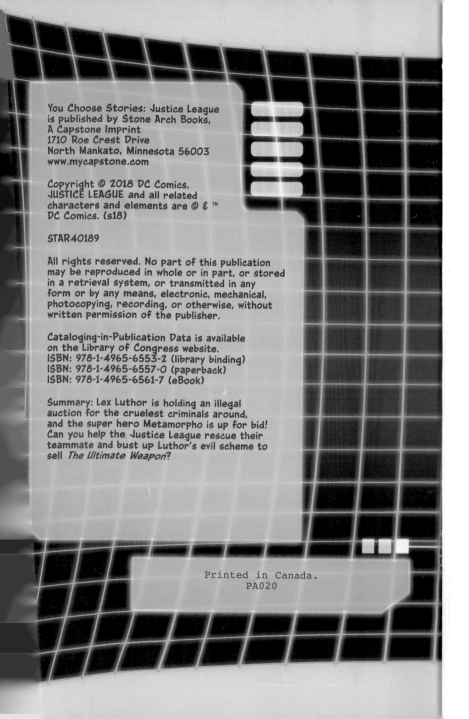

You Choose Stories: Justice League
is published by Stone Arch Books,
A Capstone Imprint
1710 Roe Crest Drive
North Mankato, Minnesota 56003
www.mycapstone.com

STAR40189

Cataloging-in-Publication Data is available
on the Library of Congress website.
ISBN: 978-1-4965-6553-2 (library binding)
ISBN: 978-1-4965-6557-0 (paperback)
ISBN: 978-1-4965-6561-7 (eBook)

Summary: Lex Luthor is holding an illegal
auction for the cruelest criminals around,
and the super hero Metamorpho is up for bid!
Can you help the Justice League rescue their
teammate and bust up Luthor's evil scheme to
sell *The Ultimate Weapon*?

Printed in Canada.
PA020

W9-AMS-883

DC SUPER HEROES

←YOU CHOOSE→

JUSTICE LEAGUE™

THE ULTIMATE WEAPON

written by
Matthew K. Manning

illustrated by
Erik Doescher

STONE ARCH BOOKS
a capstone imprint

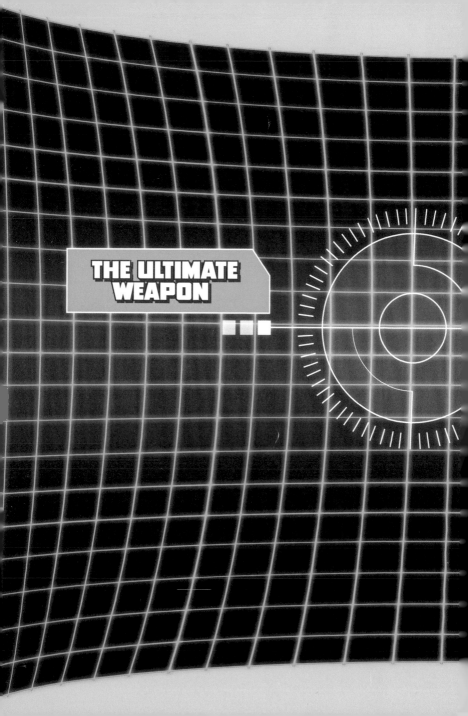

THE ULTIMATE WEAPON

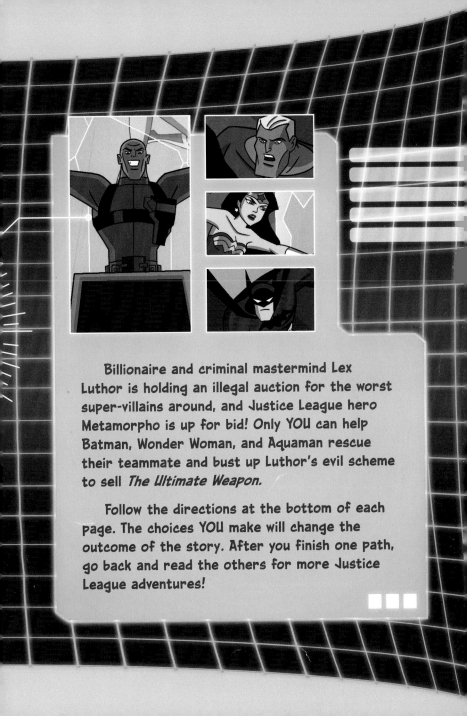

Billionaire and criminal mastermind Lex Luthor is holding an illegal auction for the worst super-villains around, and Justice League hero Metamorpho is up for bid! Only YOU can help Batman, Wonder Woman, and Aquaman rescue their teammate and bust up Luthor's evil scheme to sell *The Ultimate Weapon*.

Follow the directions at the bottom of each page. The choices YOU make will change the outcome of the story. After you finish one path, go back and read the others for more Justice League adventures!

"If this is so important, where's Batman?" Aquaman says. His voice is impatient.

Batman sent out the order to meet on this Gotham City rooftop. As the king of the underwater city of Atlantis, Aquaman isn't used to taking orders from anyone. He also isn't used to waiting, which is what he and Wonder Woman have been doing for the last five minutes.

Wonder Woman looks across the dark rooftop at her teammate. "Batman has been here for three minutes," she says.

"What?" says Aquaman.

Wonder Woman nods toward the rooftop's stairwell. Aquaman narrows his eyes as a shadow moves in the darkness.

"It's time," Batman says, stepping into the moonlight.

"How—" Aquaman begins to ask.

"Trade secret," Batman says.

Turn the page.

Aquaman watches Batman walk to the edge of the rooftop. The Sea King is still confused. With his enhanced vision, he can see into the darkest parts of the ocean. Yet he couldn't spot this man in a Batsuit hiding just a few feet away from him.

"There," Batman says suddenly.

Down on the street below, a man in a brown suit with a matching bowler hat walks out the back exit of a store. Aquaman doesn't recognize him. But Batman seems to.

"Clock King," Wonder Woman whispers. Apparently she knows the man as well.

Batman doesn't say anything. He just shoots his grapnel and swings to the next building.

"You think he's ever going to tell us why we're here?" Aquaman says to Wonder Woman.

She simply smiles and then leaps off the roof.

Aquaman follows behind. He and Wonder Woman have no trouble keeping up with Batman. They both have super-strength. They easily jump from building to building.

A few dozen rooftops later, Batman stops. Wonder Woman and Aquaman land next to him.

"We're here," the Dark Knight says.

Aquaman looks over the building's edge. Clock King stands in an alleyway. He nervously glances both ways down the small street. The villain is checking to see if anyone has followed him.

Unfortunately for Clock King, he doesn't think to look up. Instead, he knocks on the steel door in front of him. A slot in the door slides open.

"Chemistry," says Clock King.

Click. The door unlocks.

"Batman," Wonder Woman says in a stern voice. "What's this all about? Since when is someone like Clock King worth calling in the Justice League?"

"Lex Luthor is auctioning something off to criminals tonight," Batman explains. "Clock King was invited."

"So what's up for bid?" Aquaman asks.

Turn the page.

"My sources only say that Luthor is calling it 'the ultimate weapon,'" Batman replies.

"That can't be good," says Wonder Woman.

"No," says Batman. "So we better get dressed for the occasion."

He opens his cape to reveal a duffel bag.

Aquaman stares at it. First he didn't see Batman on the roof. How did he not notice that his teammate was carrying such a large bag?

Batman sees Aquaman's confused look. "Trade secret," he says again. He reaches into the bag and pulls out bundles of clothes for each of them.

A few minutes later, Wonder Woman steps out from behind the building's chimney. Only she no longer looks like her heroic self. She's wearing the purple and black uniform of the Green Lantern villain known as Star Sapphire.

"You're too tall," says Batman. "But they won't notice."

"I can't believe you're making me wear this," says Aquaman as he comes over.

The Sea King is now in the black and gray uniform of one of his greatest enemies, Black Manta. His voice sounds electronic underneath the big helmet.

"We're all making sacrifices," says Batman.

He steps into the light to reveal his own disguise. He's dressed in the half black, half white suit of Two-Face. Batman's makeup is perfect, down to the most minor details of the villain's half-scarred face.

The transformation is almost unbelievable. Wonder Woman has to hold in a gasp. Aquaman doesn't manage to do the same.

The three disguised super heroes jump down into the dark alleyway.

Batman knocks on the steel door. "Chemistry," he says.

The slot slides open to reveal a pair of dark eyes. But the eyes don't see the Dark Knight. They see Two-Face, Star Sapphire, and Black Manta.

Click.

Turn the page.

Batman opens the unlocked door. He and his teammates walk down a dimly lit hallway until they enter a large room. It's crowded with some of the biggest names in the super-villain world.

The Joker. Mr. Freeze. Captain Boomerang. The Riddler. Cheetah. Trickster. Captain Cold. And many more.

"Do I have an opening bid on the ultimate weapon?" says Lex Luthor from behind a podium on the stage.

The villain gestures to the tall tank beside him. It's full of green liquid. Inside floats a body.

"Metamorpho!" Aquaman whispers. "They've captured our teammate and put him up for bid!"

Batman shares his surprise. This situation just got serious. Metamorpho can shift his body into any combination of elements found in the human body. He's one of the most dangerous super heroes alive. The League needs to rescue their teammate—fast.

If the Justice League members attack, turn to page 13.
If they wait to catch the highest bidder, turn to page 14.
If they bid on Metamorpho, turn to page 16.

Aquaman immediately leaps onto the stage. He punches Metamorpho's tank with all his strength. But the special glass doesn't crack.

Wonder Woman shakes her head. The Sea King has rushed into action without thinking. He's outed them to a room full of criminals!

Suddenly, Wonder Woman feels a sharp pain in the back of her head. Everything goes black.

When she wakes up, she tries to move. But her arms are chained. She spots Batman and Aquaman unconscious on either side of her. All three heroes are chained to the back wall of the stage. None of them have on their villain disguises. Wonder Woman briefly wonders how Batman wore his cowl under all that Two-Face makeup.

"As I was saying before we were so rudely interrupted," says Lex Luthor from behind the podium. "Do I have an opening bid?"

Wonder Woman makes a fist. She knows these chains can't hold her. She can escape, but she'll only have time to free one of her teammates.

If Wonder Woman tries to free Batman, turn to page 18.
If Wonder Woman tries to free Aquaman, turn to page 25.

Batman glances at Aquaman. He can't see his teammate's face behind the Black Manta helmet. But Aquaman looks ready to attack.

"Wait," Batman says under his breath.

Even whispering, Batman uses his best Two-Face voice. He's not about to break character and battle a room full of super-villains. The best plan is to wait until the auction is finished. They can go after the winner once he or she is alone.

Aquaman pauses. Then his body relaxes. He takes a half step backward.

The heroes focus on the auction once again.

"Ten million dollars!" yells the Riddler.

For a second, Batman wonders where the villain came across that much cash. It was certainly not here in Gotham City. Not on his watch.

But the thought lasts only that brief moment. Because that's when the ceiling caves in.

KABOOOOOOOM!!!

Batman immediately leaps to the side. Wonder Woman jumps too, but quicker. She even manages to knock Aquaman out of the way of the falling ceiling.

Most of the villains aren't as fast. The few who are still conscious look up in complete surprise.

The powerful alien tyrant named Mongul drops down from his spaceship hovering above the building. He lands on the destroyed stage.

"I will take this 'weapon,' Luthor," Mongul says.

Lex Luthor stands behind his podium. A force field glows around him. He's untouched by the ceiling rubble. Luthor knows it's important to plan for every possibility.

"Be my guest," Luthor replies in a calm voice. He also knows when to live and fight another day.

Mongul takes Metamorpho's tank under his arm and prepares to leap out of the building. The Justice League members are left wondering what they should do next.

If the heroes follow Mongul, turn to page 20.
If the trio attacks Mongul directly, turn to page 27.

If the Justice League wants Metamorpho back, the simplest way is to pay for him. Or at least go through the motions.

"One hundred million dollars," Batman bids in his best Two-Face voice.

"Well, well. Harvey Dent," says Lex Luthor from behind the podium. "Where does a second-stringer like you get that kind of money?"

"He has partners," says Aquaman. His voice is electronic from inside the Black Manta helmet. "Partners with plenty of lost gold taken from shipwrecks."

Lex Luthor smiles. "One hundred million it is."

BOOM!

Every eye turns toward the back of the room as a large glowing portal suddenly appears. It's a Boom Tube, a teleportation system that lets beings take shortcuts through space. Whatever comes through probably won't be good.

"One _billion_ of your Earth dollars," says a deep voice from inside the Boom Tube.

"You were not invited," says Luthor from behind the podium.

Luthor knows that shadowy figure. It's the ruler of a planet called Apokolips—the ruthless alien Darkseid. He's one of the most dangerous beings in the universe.

The stone-faced Darkseid steps out of the Boom Tube and starts walking through the crowd. The super-villains part as he heads toward the stage. No one is foolish enough to stand in Darkseid's way.

"That's correct. And I'll let you in on another secret," says Darkseid. He smiles. "I'm not really bidding, either. Your Metamorpho, as you call him, might help me unlock the secret of the Anti-Life Equation. It is my life's work. So I will simply take him from you."

Batman looks at Wonder Woman and Aquaman. If they're going to act, they have to do it quickly.

If the heroes attack Darkseid, turn to page 23.
If they remain hidden among the crowd, turn to page 29.

Wonder Woman knows she has to act quickly. Batman has always been the planner in the group. If they want to stand a chance of getting away, he's the obvious choice. Luckily, no one has noticed she's awake.

"One million!" shouts a voice from the crowd.

Luthor laughs. "Come now," he says. "I think we can do better than that. After all, this auction is for the whole lot of heroes—Wonder Woman, Batman, Aquaman, *and* Metamorpho. The winner does with them what he or she will."

"One billion smackeroos!" yells another voice. It sounds like a certain white-faced criminal clown.

"That's more like it," says Luthor.

All the eyes in the room turn to the Joker as he lets out his trademark laugh. So Wonder Woman takes the opportunity to snap her chains.

Then she breaks the metal around Batman's wrists. She grabs the unconscious hero and charges toward the wall at the back of the stage.

CRRRRAAAAASH!

At full speed, Wonder Woman's shoulder smashes into the brick wall. The bricks easily give way to her near-invulnerable body. She lands in the back alley behind the building.

Wonder Woman can hear yells and shouts erupt from the auction hall. Soon the alley will be flooded with some of the most powerful super-villains in the world. She has to get out of there. She has to retreat.

"Batcave," says a weak voice.

Wonder Woman looks down at Batman. He's awake.

"Batcave," he repeats.

"But we're close to a Justice League safe house," Wonder Woman says as she jumps into the air and flies to a nearby rooftop. "We can go there to regroup."

"No," says Batman. "Batcave."

If Wonder Woman heads to the safe house, turn to page 32.
If Wonder Woman goes to the Batcave, turn to page 48.

"Star Sapphire" looks at "Black Manta," who in turn looks at "Two-Face." There's no question about it. They need to follow Mongul.

Still wearing his Two-Face costume, Batman hurries out of the auction hall and down the hallway. Wonder Woman and Aquaman follow. When they're outside, Batman reaches into his black-and-white suit. He takes out a grapnel from his Utility Belt.

Even dressed as Two-Face, Batman comes prepared.

Batman looks up at the large spaceship hovering above the building. He's about to fire the grapnel. But Wonder Woman holds out a hand.

"My way is faster," she says.

She takes Batman's hand in her own. Then she takes Aquaman's hand in her other.

Wonder Woman leaps into the sky, dragging the two men behind her. If Batman hadn't been expecting it, the force could've pulled his arm right out of its socket!

Turn to page 22.

"You're up, Aquaman," Wonder Woman says. She hurls him forward.

The Sea King holds both arms above his head. He makes two tight fists as he rockets through the air like a submarine missile.

BOOM!

Aquaman pierces the thick hull of the ship. Seconds later, Wonder Woman flies through the hole. She pulls Batman along and lands inside.

"I'll be honest," says a deep voice behind them. The heroes turn to see the huge alien Mongul. "I didn't expect a rescue effort from Earth's so-called super-villains. But . . . I can always use three more gladiators in my great games. What say you?"

Batman locks eyes with Wonder Woman. They've heard of Mongul's gladiatorial "games" that take place on the artificial planet called Warworld. Two people enter. Only one leaves. But could they ever agree to participate?

If the heroes agree to fight in the games, turn to page 34.
If they refuse Mongul's offer, turn to page 52.

"Diana," Batman whispers to Wonder Woman.

She nods. She knows that tone. Without a word, Wonder Woman peels off the Star Sapphire mask and hovers into the air. Then she flies directly toward Darkseid at full speed.

CRUNCH!

Her fists strike the villain's stone-like skin. The punch sends him hurtling toward the back of the room.

In the few seconds it takes for Wonder Woman to attack Darkseid, Batman has switched out of his Two-Face costume. Aquaman looks over at him.

"Hey, you can even do that without a phone booth," Aquaman says.

Batman doesn't respond as Aquaman takes off the Black Manta helmet. The Dark Knight has other things to focus on—including the dozens of super-villains currently watching the heroes' every move. They look on in a mix of shock and anger.

Turn the page.

Unlike the other criminals, Lex Luthor looks calm. He's completely recovered from the surprise of Darkseid's invasion and the sudden reveal of the three heroes.

"It looks like you people need a hand with Darkseid," Luthor says to Batman from the stage. He waves a hand toward the crowd. "I could help. Just say the word, Dark Knight Detective. You'll have an army of villains at your side."

Batman clenches his jaw. He looks across the large auction hall. Wonder Woman punches Darkseid again. The alien is stunned, but for how long?

The hero doesn't think he can trust Lex Luthor. Luthor is one of Superman's worst enemies, and he has carried out hundreds of evil plans. But now, Batman is faced with an even more powerful foe. Is the enemy of his enemy now his friend?

Batman is not sure he has much of a choice.

If Batman teams up with the super-villains, turn to page 36.
If the Dark Knight distrusts Lex Luthor, turn to page 55.

"One billion and a quarter!" shouts the Joker from the front row. Next to him, Harley Quinn giggles.

"You tell 'em, Mr. J!" Harley says.

Wonder Woman looks at the size of the crowd. If she needed a carefully thought-out plan, Batman would be the clear choice. But she doesn't need strategy at the moment. With this many super-villains, she needs muscle. So she must free Aquaman.

The hero works quickly.

Ching

Wonder Woman pulld with all her might and pops her first chain.

Ching

She breaks the second. She immediately does the same for the unconscious Sea King.

Turn the page.

"Ugh," Aquaman groans.

He slowly opens his eyes. He looks out at the crowd as he leans against Wonder Woman for balance.

"Um, are they supposed to be all loose like that?" Harley Quinn says, pointing up to the stage.

Lex Luthor turns around. His eyes widen. Then he turns back to face his audience.

"If you don't want your prizes getting away, I'd do something," Luthor says in a surprisingly calm voice. "Now."

Aquaman feels Wonder Woman tug at his arm. She's getting ready to leave.

The Sea King doesn't move. He knows this situation is his fault. He attacked without thinking things through. So now he's the one who has to fix this mess.

If Aquaman flees the scene with Wonder Woman, turn to page 68.

If Aquaman tries to free Metamorpho, turn to page 85.

Shink! Shink!

Two Batarangs strike Metamorpho's tank.

Mongul looks down at the large tank under his arm. Tiny cracks have appeared where the weapons hit.

The villain frowns. Mongul knows the weapons are Batarangs, but Batman shouldn't be at this auction. His thorough research would have revealed as much.

Nevertheless, Mongul leaps out of the building with his prize.

Pfft!

The line from Batman's grapnel shoots off and wraps itself around Mongul's leg. As the alien soars out through the hole in the roof, he pulls Batman with him.

Mongul lands safely inside his spaceship's open launching bay. The massive door begins to close behind him. Batman swings inside just as it slams shut.

Turn the page.

Mongul turns and looks at the man standing across from him. "You are not the one they call Two-Face," he says. "It's a nice disguise, *Batman*. But ultimately pointless."

THUNK!

Something strikes the ship from outside. Mongul loses his balance as the spacecraft dips to the right. Batman remains unmoved. It's as if he was expecting the attack.

THUNK!

The ship surges again. Suddenly, red lights flood the chamber.

"I don't know who your allies are," says Mongul. "But they seem to be crashing my ship."

Batman smiles. "They tend to do things like that," he replies.

But despite his smile, the Dark Knight is worried. Wonder Woman is doing more damage to the spaceship than he expected. Was coming onto the vessel the right course of action?

If Batman stays aboard the ship, turn to page 71.
If Batman tries to leave, turn to page 88.

Wonder Woman lurches forward and gets ready to attack. But Batman holds out his arm.

"No," he says.

"I'm not asking for permission," says Wonder Woman beneath her Star Sapphire costume. She knows Darkseid. She knows the damage he can do.

"Wait," Batman says. "Trust me."

Wonder Woman locks eyes with the man dressed as Two-Face. Then she lets herself relax. Just slightly.

The heroes turn their attention back to the stage. Lex Luthor stares down Darkseid.

"This item is not free for the taking," says the billionaire from behind his podium. "If you're not going to make a bid, I must ask you to leave."

Darkseid doesn't say anything. He simply laughs.

Turn the page.

Lex Luthor narrows his eyes. He's not used to the obvious disrespect that Darkseid is showing him.

"Fine," Luthor says. "If you're going to be stubborn about it, I'll show you the door myself."

Luthor pulls out a small box from underneath the podium. He presses a button on the device. Suddenly, the open Boom Tube behind Darkseid begins to suck in air. Within seconds, the powerful foe and a handful of nearby villains are pulled in through the portal.

BOOM!

The Boom Tube closes. Darkseid is gone.

"Now," says Lex Luthor, as if nothing out of the ordinary happened. "The bid was at one hundred million, if I'm not mistaken."

Batman is surprised Luthor was able to get rid of Darkseid so easily. The billionaire is more of a threat than he realized. Is it wise to stay here?

If Batman continues to bid, turn to page 73.
If the heroes leave to get backup, turn to page 91.

Batman is often right, but so is Wonder Woman. And she's already made up her mind. "It's my call," she says. "We're going to the Justice League safe house."

Wonder Woman starts to move again, but she can see from the scowl on Batman's face that he's not a fan of being carried. So she sets him down on the rooftop. He cringes in pain when he puts weight on his leg.

"You're hurt," Wonder Woman says.

"I'm fine," Batman replies.

"No," she says. "You're anything but—"

SKOOOOOOOOM

Batman barely manages to dive out of the way as a blast of ice hurtles past him. Wonder Woman looks over at the building across the street. Captain Cold is standing on its roof.

His cold gun is aimed directly at her.

SKOOOOOOOOM

Wonder Woman crosses her bracelets in front of her face.

BZZZIIIING!

The frosty blast bounces off her metal bracelets and back toward the villain.

"Run!" Wonder Woman yells at Batman.

She knows she could handle Captain Cold in a fight. However, it won't take long for more super-villains from the auction to join him. With only an injured Batman by her side, she can't hope to take on all of them.

Batman doesn't argue. He limps quickly toward the other end of the rooftop. He spreads out his cape.

Then he simply steps off the roof.

By the time Wonder Woman reaches the ledge, the Dark Knight is already swinging down the block on his grapnel's line.

Turn to page 38.

Batman looks past Mongul and around the large chamber of the alien tyrant's spaceship. There's no sign of Metamorpho. A simple smash-and-grab rescue is out of the question. They need to play along for now. They need to agree to fight in Mongul's games.

"All right," Batman says. He speaks in his best Two-Face voice. "We'll fight, but on one condition."

"You want the one called Metamorpho," says Mongul. "For some pathetic revenge scheme against the Justice League, no doubt."

"Yes," growls Batman.

Mongul grins. The expression worries the Dark Knight. This intergalactic villain is obviously up to something.

"I think that can be arranged," Mongul says.

* * *

A full day passes before Mongul schedules the gladiatorial fight.

For the heroes, that day is almost pleasant. The alien ship brought Batman, Wonder Woman, and Aquaman to the gigantic artificial metal planet called Warworld. Then the disguised heroes were given large individual rooms with soft beds. They were well fed with rare fruits and tasty meals. They were treated to relaxing massages.

All the while, Batman's mind raced. He looked for ways to escape. His eyes searched every room for Metamorpho. Yet he didn't break character as Two-Face. All three heroes managed to keep their secrets safe.

But now, as day turns to night, the pampering ends. Three large alien creatures arrive at Batman's room.

"Up," one says in crude English. "Up now!"

Batman does as he's told. He stands and puts on his half black, half white jacket. Then he follows the aliens down a dark hallway and into a brightly lit arena.

Turn to page 42.

"Save it, Luthor. We'd never—" begins Aquaman.

"Deal," Batman says.

Aquaman turns to look at his teammate. "We're teaming up with super-villains now?" he exclaims.

"It's three of us versus Darkseid," Batman says. "You do the math."

Aquaman shrugs and then shoves his way through the crowd of confused villains. He heads toward the back of the room. Wonder Woman is still there, walloping a dazed Darkseid. Meanwhile Batman hurries to the stage.

"Give me a moment to rally the troops," Luthor tells the hero in a bored voice.

"First, I'll be taking your 'ultimate weapon,'" Batman says.

Luthor grins. "Anything for a friend."

The Dark Knight steps over to Metamorpho's tank and gets to work. It takes him less than a minute to figure out how to free his teammate.

"Thanks, Bats," Metamorpho says as he pulls himself out of the tank and stands on the stage. He looks out at the room of villains. "What's going on here?"

Across the room, Darkseid has regained his senses and his footing. Wonder Woman's attacks are no longer having the same effect. With a powerful slap, he catches her off-guard and sends her flying.

CRRRRAAAAASSSSSHH!

Batman and Metamorpho duck as Wonder Woman shoots past and smashes into the stage.

Aquaman dives at Darkseid's legs. The alien stumbles, but he doesn't lose his balance.

"Come!" Luthor calls to the crowd. "Let's help our Justice League allies! We can't have them fighting all by themselves."

At Luthor's urging, the super-villains gain a bit of courage. They move closer to Darkseid to launch their own attacks. They fear the alien, but they might fear Luthor almost as much.

Turn to page 46.

Wonder Woman leaps into the night sky to follow Batman. She glides through the air.

SKOOOOOOOOM

Another ice blast shoots over the hero's shoulder. Captain Cold must still have her in his sights. She increases her speed.

Wonder Woman lands on the street and follows Batman around a corner. The Justice League safe house is just a few blocks away. If they can get to its secret entrance, they'll be safe. They can call in the rest of the League.

SKOOOOOOOOM

Ice suddenly covers the corner of the building. The chilly blast missed Wonder Woman by less than a foot this time. For the villain to get this close, Wonder Woman must be distracted. She shakes her head and tries to focus.

"Get down!" Batman yells suddenly.

The Dark Knight jumps out from the nearby shadows. He pushes Wonder Woman to the side just as another icy blast parts the air.

SKOOOOOOOOM

Wonder Woman hits the ground. She looks back over her shoulder. The Dark Knight is frozen solid in his tracks.

Then she looks past her teammate and down the dark street. Captain Cold is perched on a rooftop. Captain Boomerang and Trickster stand by him. The yellow ring-powered Sinestro lands next to the trio of crooks. The super-villains are catching up to her. More will arrive by the second.

Wonder Woman gets to her feet and darts in the direction of the safe house. She pumps her arms and legs. Her tremendous speed gives her quite the lead on the criminals. She should be home free. That's the thought that runs through her head as she turns another corner.

But when she sees the villain Mr. Freeze standing at the end of the alleyway, it's already too late.

SKOOOOOOOOM

Turn the page.

Later, when she awakes, Wonder Woman can't hear much through the solid sheet of ice that covers her.

Through the thick and blurry frozen shell, she can make out the large crowd in front of her. She can just see Batman out the side of her left eye. He's still trapped in his own block of ice. Out of her right eye, she sees Aquaman chained next to the tank holding Metamorpho.

Lex Luthor stands on the stage in front of her. Once more, he has taken his place behind the podium. She knows Luthor has started the auction again.

Even though she can barely feel her hand in the freezing cold, Wonder Woman manages to make a fist. She has very little hope left.

But nevertheless, the ice starts to crack.

The End

To follow another path, turn to page 12.

"This next fight is bound to be an enjoyable one," Mongul's voice booms over a loud speaker.

Batman looks up at the stadium seating all around him. Thousands of spectators are here to watch the battle. None look human. Mongul stands on a balcony, towering far overhead in special box seating. The alien tyrant is surrounded by guards.

Then Batman's attention turns toward the doors opening on either side of him. Wonder Woman and Aquaman enter the stadium. Both are still dressed as super-villains.

"I'd like to you to meet three of Earth's worst criminals," says Mongul to the crowd. "They want the hero known as Metamorpho."

A gate opens at the far side of the arena. A confused Metamorpho steps through.

"But let's see what he has to say about that, shall we?" Mongul says.

Metamorpho sees the three "villains" standing across from him. He frowns. Then he transforms his hand into a giant hammer and rushes forward.

Batman leaps out of the way of the metal hammer. But Metamorpho is able to turn into any combination of elements. So his hammer quickly forms into an iron shovel. He digs at the ground below Aquaman and hurls him across the arena.

"Stop this!" Wonder Woman says.

She throws a punch just as Metamorpho turns into a clear gas. Wonder Woman's fist passes through the invisible cloud.

Metamorpho transforms back into his human form and makes his arm into a golden sword. He thrusts the blade forward. The Dark Knight dodges it and steps in closer.

"Rex," Batman whispers. "It's me."

Metamorpho pauses. Two-Face doesn't know his secret identity is Rex Mason. And that voice certainly doesn't belong to Two-Face. That voice belongs to his friend, Batman.

"Plan?" Metamorpho asks as he pretends to take another stab.

"Let's take the fight to Mongul," Batman says.

Turn the page.

Batman glances over at Aquaman and Wonder Woman. He gives a small nod.

Metamorpho fakes an attack. He grabs Aquaman and flings him toward the box seats of Mongul and his guards. Then Metamorpho leaps into the air after his "opponent."

At that same moment, Wonder Woman swoops over to Batman and grabs him. She lifts him up and flies at top speed toward Mongul.

In seconds, they all reach the alien tyrant's box seat.

Metamorpho lashes out with an arm shaped into a cobalt hammer. Wonder Woman punches Mongul under his jaw. Batman breaks a knockout capsule in the villain's face. And Aquaman delivers a powerful hit to Mongul's stomach.

All the attacks land at the same exact moment. It's the result of countless training sessions. It's an attack a hero and three villains would never be able to pull off.

It's an attack Mongul is simply unprepared for.

WHOMP!

Mongul hits the floor of his balcony. He was unconscious before he even began to fall. The guards look down at their leader, and then at the heroes. They raise their weapons.

"I wouldn't, if I were you," says Batman.

They just as quickly lower their weapons. Batman smiles beneath his Two-Face makeup.

"Warworld's hangar is close by," Batman says to the other heroes. "We can grab a spaceship there. We need to leave before Mongul wakes up."

It takes the teammates less than fifteen minutes to find the hangar and make their way off of Warworld. Mongul doesn't wake up for another hour after that.

By then, the Justice League is long gone. There's nothing left for the weakened Mongul to do but go back to sleep. Dreams of victory are now his only option.

The End

To follow another path, turn to page 12.

The Cheetah scratches at Darkseid's face. Weather Wizard shoots a lightning bolt. Solomon Grundy grabs Darkseid's arms from behind. For a brief moment, it looks as if the villains might be able to beat their mighty foe.

But the moment passes.

"Is this enough people, Darkseid?" Luthor asks. "I know I promised you there would be more heroes, but they're such an unpredictable bunch."

Batman turns toward the podium to stare at the evil billionaire. He realizes what's happening, but it's too late. Luthor has outsmarted him.

Suddenly Darkseid straightens up. He easily swats away Aquaman and the super-villains. It's as if the alien hasn't been trying until now.

"This will do," says Darkseid.

BOOOOOM!

The noise is louder this time. A huge Boom Tube forms around the room. It teleports the heroes and villains before they even know what's happening.

Batman looks at his new surroundings. He sees the blood red skies of the planet known as Apokolips above. Wonder Woman, Metamorpho, Aquaman, and dozens of villains stand nearby. The only person missing is Luthor.

Because this was all Luthor's plan. He tricked villains and heroes into one room so Darkseid could easily teleport them to his home world. Once again, Lex Luthor sold out humankind without even batting an eye.

"Welcome, all," Darkseid says. "You will make an excellent group of test subjects."

A man in a purple robe steps toward Aquaman. "Yes," the man says as he studies the Sea King. "The powers of these Earthlings will make fine additions to our Parademon army, once properly absorbed. That is, I mean . . . *your* army, master."

Batman feels the chains click against his wrists. His mind begins to search for an escape plan. But this time, one doesn't come.

The End

To follow another path, turn to page 12.

SKOOOOOOOOM

An icy blast suddenly shoots by. It barely misses Wonder Woman's head. She turns around and sees Captain Cold standing on a neighboring rooftop. His cold gun is aimed at the two heroes.

"Fine. We'll go to the Batcave," Wonder Woman says. "You better be right about this, Bruce."

"When am I wrong?" Batman says in a weak voice. A smile appears on his face.

Wonder Woman takes off into the air with Batman still in her arms. A boomerang nips at her feet as she flies. There's no doubt in her mind that Captain Boomerang has now joined his fellow villain on the roof behind her.

"There," Batman says after less than a minute.

He points down at a dark alley. Wonder Woman lands. She doesn't notice the parked Batmobile until Batman pushes a button on his Utility Belt. The vehicle seems to appear out of nowhere as its cloaking system shuts off.

Batman limps over to the driver's side of the Batmobile. He doesn't say anything, but Wonder Woman can tell he's hurt. He must've been injured back at the auction house.

The Batmobile's canopy slides open. Batman smoothly jumps in, but his face reveals his pain. Wonder Woman drops herself into the passenger's seat. As the canopy closes above them, the engine roars to life.

Wonder Woman smiles. Batman is the master of secrecy and hiding in shadows, yet he makes such a noticeable spectacle out of his car. It's all just a part of his carefully planned out image, she thinks. The Batmobile is designed to strike as much fear into criminals as Batman himself.

VRRRRRROOOOOOOOOOOOOMMMMMM!

The Batmobile speeds out of the alley and onto another dirty Gotham City street. Scraps of paper blow in the wind behind it.

Turn the page.

The Batmobile races down Robinson Blvd toward the parkway. As it passes a full parking lot, one of the vehicle's headlights switches on. An old-fashioned car pulls out onto the street. It heads in the same direction as the Batmobile. The car looks like something from the 1940s, yet it's painted in a bizarre yellow and blue plaid.

"Can't this thing go any faster?" says the man in the car's passenger seat.

He wears a green hat and matching green bodysuit. On his chest is a purple question mark. There's no mistaking this foe of Batman. It's the puzzle-obsessed criminal known as the Riddler.

"Hrrm," says a deep voice from behind him.

The voice seems to be agreeing with the Riddler. Crammed into the car's back seat is the massive swamp monster called Solomon Grundy.

"Glad you asked!" exclaims the man behind the wheel. He's dressed in colors that match his car.

Turn to page 60.

"We won't be your puppets, Mongul!" says Wonder Woman. "We won't fight for you."

"Fools. Do you think I don't know who you are?" says Mongul. As he speaks, a few dozen of his alien guards rush into the chamber.

Wonder Woman, Batman, and Aquaman exchange worried glances.

"Metamorpho, as you call him, is of great value to me in my gladiatorial games," Mongul continues. "The games have gotten a bit stale lately. He would add much needed excitement. So I researched all the possible bidders at Luthor's pathetic auction and prepared."

He looks at each of them. "Star Sapphire, you'll find my ship vibrates on a wavelength that keeps you from using your powers. Black Manta, your armor was hacked the moment you set foot on my ship. And you, Two-Face. Well, you're as powerless as Gotham City's hero himself. You are no threat to me. Yes, I know you three villains very well."

Wonder Woman feels a wave of relief. Their secret is still safe. Mongul thinks they're simply criminals. He's not prepared to deal with the three heroes who are his actual prisoners.

"If you won't take part in my games," adds Mongul, "then you will meet the same fate as others who have tried to say no to me."

Aquaman takes a step forward. He's ready to fight, but Batman stops him with just a look. They're outnumbered. It's not the right time to act.

"Take them," Mongul says to his guards. Then he turns and walks out of the chamber.

The guards rush forward. They thrust their laser rifles at the heroes.

"Move!" a guard yells.

The three Justice League members are marched down a hallway. All the while, Batman studies his surroundings. He looks quickly through doorways. He glances down hallways.

Turn the page.

Mongul's guards shove Batman, Aquaman, and Wonder Woman into a small room with just a single metal bench.

Clang

Behind them, a large steel door slams shut.

When he's sure they're alone, Batman finally speaks. He no longer tries to talk like Two-Face. There's no point now.

"I saw Metamorpho," Batman says. "He's being held in a room two doors down from this one. There are two guards. One is asleep. The other is favoring his right leg. His left looks to be injured. Take advantage of that."

Aquaman stares at his teammate. "You know," he says. "Some days you're way more Batman-y than others."

Batman grunts in response.

"Mongul and his guards think we're powerless super-villains," Batman says. "Let's set the record straight."

Turn to page 64.

Batman completely ignores Lex Luthor's offer and turns back toward his teammate. The last thing the Justice League is going to do is work with one of the world's most corrupt billionaires. No matter how desperate the situation.

Luthor simply shrugs from behind the podium. The deal was worth a shot, at least.

"I'll get Metamorpho. You help Wonder Woman," Batman tells Aquaman.

Batman fires his grapnel toward the stage.

Pfft!

He swings above the crowd of confused super-villains. Batman's boots strike the side of Metamorpho's tank. The special glass-like material cracks.

Krrrrrrrshhhhhhhh

A greenish liquid begins to leak out of the cracks. Then the pressure becomes too much. The tank shatters, and the liquid gushes out.

Turn the page.

When the tank is empty, Metamorpho stands next to Batman on the stage.

"Whoa," says Metamorpho, looking around the auction hall. "This seems bad."

Across the room, Wonder Woman and Aquaman are taking turns punching Darkseid. Some of the super-villains watch the fight, but others are starting to notice Batman. They see him standing next to the freed "ultimate weapon" they came to bid on. The villains don't look happy about it.

"You're right," Batman says. "It is bad. Darkseid can't be here. We have enough to deal with right now."

Batman presses a button on his Utility Belt. Meanwhile, the criminals begin to step toward him and Metamorpho.

"Uh, Bats?" Metamorpho says.

But the Dark Knight isn't paying attention. He's busy typing something on a control panel on his belt.

Pfft!

Without a word, Batman fires his grapnel at the ceiling of the large room.

Metamorpho smiles as the Dark Knight lifts off the ground. He's glad Batman is ready to do something about the situation, even if he doesn't know what that something is.

The elemental hero follows Batman's lead. He turns his body to gas and hovers into the air above the super-villains.

Batman lands near Darkseid. He throws three Batarangs.

Tunk! Tunk! Tunk!

They barely stick into the alien's tough chest. Then the Batarangs begin to beep.

"Now!" shouts Wonder Woman.

She knows what's about to happen. She and Aquaman both punch Darkseid directly in the jaw. At that same moment, Metamorpho changes into his human form with a fist made out of iron. He lunges forward and gets ready to strike.

Turn the page.

Darkseid has only a second to dodge Metamorpho's attack. The villain stumbles back toward the Boom Tube behind him. It's exactly the direction the heroes want him to go.

Suddenly, the Batarangs stuck in the villain's chest explode.

BAWOOM! BAWOOM! BAWOOM!

The explosions don't hurt the powerful Darkseid, but the quick flurry of attacks has thrown him off-balance. Darkseid can no longer keep his footing. He falls back into the Boom Tube completely.

BOOM!

The tube shuts behind him. But the heroes have no time to celebrate their victory.

Batman, Aquaman, Metamorpho, and Wonder Woman turn to face a room full of super-villains. None of the crooks look pleased to see them.

"Get ready," Batman says to his teammates.

Turn to page 67.

The man in the bright blue and yellow costume slams his foot down on the pedal.

VRRRRROOOOOM!

Riddler and Solomon Grundy are both thrown back as the car goes from twenty to ninety miles per hour in a heartbeat. A large flame shoots out of the back of the car.

"Trickster!" shouts the Riddler in surprise.

"Hey," says Trickster, "it was your idea!"

The car speeds along the dark streets after the Batmobile.

"Don't get too close," says the Riddler as he straightens up in his seat. "Let's follow them and see where they go. Then . . . we can introduce them to Grundy."

"Hrrm," agrees Solomon Grundy from the back seat.

Trickster eases off the pedal just slightly. It's not a bad plan.

"Do you—?" Wonder Woman starts to say from her seat next to the Dark Knight in the Batmobile.

"See Trickster's ridiculous car following us?" says Batman. He glances up at the rearview mirror. "It would be hard to miss."

"So then why are we still headed to the Batcave?" Wonder Woman asks.

She knows this road. It leads fourteen miles outside of Gotham City to Wayne Manor. One turn later, and they'd be driving into the caves below that hide all of Batman's secrets.

Batman just smiles. "*Is* that where we're headed?"

Wonder Woman knows the situation is serious. But she can't help but grin too—even as the Batmobile pulls off the road and straight through the wall of a cliffside.

Turn the page.

"How is that possible?" asks the Riddler.

As always, the villain is searching for an answer. The Riddler just saw the Batmobile disappear into solid rock as clearly as he can see the other two people in Trickster's car.

"The cliff is a hologram. It has to be," says Trickster. "Boys, it's our lucky day. I think we found the Batcave!"

Trickster swerves his car to the right. He heads directly for the gray rock. But instead of smashing into boulders, the cliffside disappears. They drive safely through the hologram and into the Batcave.

The Riddler frowns as he looks at the high-tech equipment all around the cave. "That's what I mean," he says. "How could Batman be so careless? It's like he just let us find this place."

Before Trickster can answer, something lifts his car into the air. The vehicle smashes into the cave's ceiling.

CRASH!

After the car hurtles back down to the ground, the Riddler climbs out of the wreckage. Trickster and Solomon Grundy are still inside. They're both unconscious from the crash.

"When is a Batcave like a Riddler?" says Wonder Woman. The hero stands in front of the criminal. She lifts him up by the back of his costume. It's much easier than lifting Trickster's car had been.

"When it's a dummy," mutters the Riddler. Then his eyes roll back as he passes out. The stress is just too much for the weak villain.

"Wow," says Wonder Woman to Batman as he limps out of the shadows. "He figured that one out pretty quickly."

Batman doesn't reply. He walks toward the Batmobile. It's parked farther inside the fake Batcave. He calls the rest of the Justice League on the Batmobile's radio and sends out the location of the auction house. Then he closes his eyes and allows himself a moment's rest.

The End

To follow another path, turn to page 12.

Wonder Woman easily lifts the heavy steel door to their prison cell. Aquaman and Batman rush out first. Wonder Woman follows.

Clang

The door crashes back into place as they run through the halls. None of the heroes even flinch. They're too focused on the mission. Soon they reach the room holding Metamorpho.

TUNK! TUNK! TUNK!

Aquaman punches the door open with three well-placed strikes. Batman runs inside. He sweeps the awake guard's injured leg out from under him.

The sleeping guard stirs, and his eyes open. Before he can act, Wonder Woman lifts him up and hurls him at Metamorpho's tank.

The guard is knocked back into unconsciousness as he shatters the thick glass.

Kssssssshhhhhhh!

"Uhhh," groans Metamorpho. He slumps forward as the liquid pours out of the tank.

Batman puts Metamorpho's arm over his shoulder. He helps the elemental hero to his feet.

"Two-Face?" Metamorpho weakly mutters.

"More guards are on their way," Aquaman says from the doorway.

Wonder Woman rushes over to the Sea King. She looks down the hall. A dozen yellow aliens charge forward. Each one looks larger than the one before.

"I don't understand," says Metamorpho. He struggles to stay standing. "What's going on?"

"It's OK. We're—" Batman starts to say, but he's interrupted when a laser shoots by his head. It misses him by less than an inch.

BZOOOM! BZOOOM! BZOOOM!

The guards are attacking. Some of their shots blast through the walls of the room.

Metamorpho looks at the disguised Batman. Then he looks at Wonder Woman and Aquaman.

Then he disappears.

Turn the page.

"Rex!" Batman yells as a clear gas goes up his nose. "It's not . . . what . . ."

But Batman never finishes his sentence. He passes out from the fast-acting knock-out gas Metamorpho has just changed himself into.

Metamorpho floats over to Wonder Woman. But he doesn't see his teammate. He only sees the villain Star Sapphire. Wonder Woman breathes him in without realizing it and passes out.

Metamorpho moves onto the next "villain." The Black Manta suit functions have been shut down by Mongul's ship. So Metamorpho easily enters the suit's breathing system and knocks out Aquaman.

Still confused and panicked, Metamorpho attacks the aliens next. By the time he's finished, the hero is too weak to escape. He turns back to his human form just to fall to the floor.

When he wakes, Metamorpho will still be Mongul's prisoner. And so will his own Justice League teammates whom he just helped defeat.

The End

To follow another path, turn to page 12.

"I'd like to begin by thanking you for getting rid of the elephant in the room," says the Joker. He steps toward the heroes. "Now if we could just do something about the bat problem."

The Clown Prince of Crime removes a large, cartoonish gun from his jacket pocket.

Wonder Woman quickly steps in front of Batman. The Dark Knight is many things, but invulnerable is not one of them.

But when she glances back at her teammate, Batman doesn't look worried.

KARRUNCH!

Suddenly, a giant green hand rips off the roof of the building.

Wonder Woman realizes now why Batman seemed so calm. In the air above them hovers Green Lantern—plus two dozen of the Justice League's best and brightest.

Before she can even ask how or when he sent out the call for help, Batman says, "Trade secret."

The End

To follow another path, turn to page 12.

But Aquaman is just too weak for a fight. He's been out of water for too long. His body is never working at its best when he's out of his natural element.

So he lets Wonder Woman help him limp offstage.

Wonder Woman moves quickly. She can hear dozens of super-villains following them backstage.

"There's a Justice League safe house nearby," Wonder Woman says quietly.

Aquaman nods. He understands. They can't possibly take on all these criminals alone. They need to get out of the auction hall and call for backup.

"Ah!" Wonder Woman yells suddenly.

Aquaman looks down and sees a glowing yellow capture claw made entirely out of energy. It's gripping Wonder Woman's ankle. It tugs at her viciously.

Turn to page 70.

The yellow claw drags Wonder Woman away from Aquaman. The Sea King loses his balance and topples to the floor.

He turns to see Sinestro, the Yellow Lantern. The villain is using his power ring to form the claw. Sinestro pulls Wonder Woman over, and then he traps her in a large bubble of energy. Wonder Woman punches the yellow bubble as hard as she can. It doesn't budge.

In a normal fight, Aquaman would rush Sinestro. He would attempt to break the villain's focus to allow his teammate to escape. But Aquaman can barely walk, let alone fight. And Wonder Woman sees it in his face.

"Go!" she yells. Her voice is as firm and calm as ever. Even when captured, Wonder Woman remains in control.

Aquaman agrees without even realizing what he's doing. He turns and limps quickly to the back-door exit.

Turn to page 76.

Batman decides to stay on the spaceship. He can't let Mongul slip through his fingers, or risk the life of his friend Metamorpho to chance.

The ship continues to shake. Years of training allow Batman to keep his balance. The giant alien isn't so skilled. As the ship goes into a dive toward Gotham Harbor, Mongul tumbles to the other side of the chamber. Unfortunately, Metamorpho's tank rolls along with him.

Rrrrrrrrrrrrrrnnnnnnnnnkkkk

Batman looks at the bay door. It's been ripped open, and the rush of wind pulls him toward it.

The Dark Knight's reactions are as fast as ever. He draws two claw-like hand grips from his Utility Belt. They scrape against the chamber's metal wall, barely holding his weight. But they do hold and keep him from falling out of the opening.

"Hello, Batman," Wonder Woman says casually. She's no longer disguised as Star Sapphire, and she holds open the heavy bay door.

"Metamorpho!" Batman yells in response.

Turn the page.

Wonder Woman looks over. She sees Metamorpho's tank slip from Mongul's grip.

"On it!" she calls to Batman.

The tank rolls past Wonder Woman and outside the ship. She lets go of the door to dive after it.

Mongul hurls himself through the opening too. But the villain isn't chasing the tank. He no longer cares about getting the "ultimate weapon." He's only worried about his own survival now.

WHOMP!

The bay door slams shut.

Just as suddenly, the chamber returns to its normal air pressure levels. With no wind pulling at him, Batman's feet touch back on the floor.

However, the ship is still plummeting toward Gotham Harbor, and Batman sees no way to escape.

Turn to page 78.

Everyone in the room except Luthor looks stunned by the chaos of Darkseid's sudden arrival and exit. Batman knows they can't leave now. Not with all the villains so on edge. They must continue with their plan. They must continue to bid.

"Two hundred million," Batman says. His Two-Face voice is still absolutely perfect.

"You're the high bidder already," says Lex Luthor from behind the podium.

"I want to be *doubly* sure," says Batman.

Luthor sighs and then says, "Yes. Anyone else have a non-pun based bid? Do I hear three hundred million?"

"Three hundred million!" shouts the yellow ring-wearing Sinestro from the back of the room.

"Five hundred!" booms the deep voice of The Flash's foe, Gorilla Grodd.

"One billion," says Wonder Woman as she steps forward in her Star Sapphire costume.

Turn the page.

"Two-Face" turns to his teammate. He looks annoyed. It's out of character for Batman. But it's exactly what the real villain would do.

"Two billion," he snarls.

"Five billion!" Wonder Woman shouts angrily.

Aquaman steps over. Still in his Black Manta disguise, he looks threatening. He stands right in Wonder Woman's face. As far as anyone knows, he's working with Two-Face. Now it looks as if Black Manta is finally getting into the argument.

"Now, now," says Lex Luthor. "Please, let's keep this civil."

Batman reaches into the half black, half white suit jacket. "I'm of two minds on the subject," he says.

Ping

Batman flips an exact copy of Two-Face's signature coin. The villain never makes a decision without it. It lands in his palm. The scarred face is up.

Batman looks at Aquaman, then Wonder Woman. Every super-villain in the auction hall is watching the trio. But they don't see three Justice League members in a carefully planned act. They see Two-Face and his current partner, Black Manta, going up against Star Sapphire.

Batman nods.

ZAAAAAAP!

Aquaman fires Black Manta's laser beam eyes. The energy rips through the air. Still in her Star Sapphire disguise, Wonder Woman easily dodges the attack. The lasers strike the podium on the stage instead.

Lex Luthor leaps away from the blast. A glowing force field instantly forms around his body to protect him. Whatever other secret weapons Luthor had hidden in his podium spark and erupt into flames.

BOOOOOM!!!

Turn to page 82.

"Raarrh!" Aquaman growls in a noise of pure pain.

He's frustrated with himself. He knows he's the reason Metamorpho is still Lex Luthor's prisoner. He's the reason Batman and Wonder Woman are now also chained up and waiting to be sold to the highest bidder.

Aquaman shakes the thoughts away as he limps out into the dark Gotham City back alley. There will be time for blaming himself later. He owes it to the others to reach the safe house and contact the rest of the Justice League.

It's his only hope. It's his *friends'* only hope.

"Oh, this is a good day," a man suddenly says from the shadows.

Aquaman knows the voice even before the person steps out into the light.

The Joker grins. "Can you believe I was ready to put down my hard-earned money for a chance at having my own Jokerized Justice League?" he says.

"I *can* believe it!" says another voice. Harley Quinn steps out of the shadows too.

"Why, since everyone else is so busy, I think I'll just take my fish to go," says the Joker. He pulls a strangely oversized gun out of his pants' waistband.

Aquaman looks at the gun, and then lunges at the Joker. But in his weakened state, the Sea King is too slow.

A puff of green smoke fills the air around Aquaman's head as the Joker fires. The hero falls to the ground. He begins to smile. Then Aquaman's smile turns into frantic laughter before he passes out, unconscious.

"I'll never get tired of this old gag," says the Joker. "Now who ordered the laughing fish?"

The End

To follow another path, turn to page 12.

Batman quickly reviews the situation.

There's no time for him to reach the ship's controls in the cockpit. And he can't lift open the heavy bay door. The ship is going to crash into Gotham Harbor—and he's going down with it.

The hero's mind is calm. Batman knew the risks and has few regrets.

* * *

Outside the ship, Wonder Woman catches Metamorpho's tank in midair. The heavy container throws her off-balance, and she tumbles through the night sky. She rights herself just as Mongul splashes nearby into Gotham Harbor.

Within seconds, Wonder Woman lands gracefully on the boardwalk lining the harbor. She sets the tank down, and turns to fly back for Batman.

But before she can lift off, she watches in horror as Mongul's ship hits the water. It explodes in a burst of flames.

Turn to page 80.

It takes Aquaman less than five minutes to pull the unconscious Mongul from Gotham Harbor. The force of the impact knocked out the super tough alien, but it didn't seem to do any permanent damage. It took all Aquaman's strength just to lift Mongul from the water.

"Any sign of Batman?" Wonder Woman asks Aquaman as he steps onto the small beach near the boardwalk.

Aquaman is now back in his regular uniform as well. He removed the Black Manta disguise in mid-dive. It was impressive that he wore the insulting costume of his archenemy for as long as he did.

"No," Aquaman says. His voice is serious. There is no joy in what he has to say. "I'll keep looking."

"That won't be necessary," says a raspy voice from behind them.

Wonder Woman and Aquaman both turn around in surprise.

Batman and Metamorpho walk out of the water and onto the beach. Neither looks injured. Wonder Women even thinks she sees a slight smile on the Dark Knight's face. Before she can say the word *how*, Batman is already talking.

"My Batarangs cracked Metamorpho's tank earlier. He slipped out by changing to a gas when we were on Mongul's ship," Batman says.

"Hey, guys," Metamorpho says with a very obvious grin.

"Before the ship crashed, Metamorpho turned himself into a high-density foam to protect me," Batman says.

"What my friend is trying to tell you is that I saved his bat-shaped behind," says Metamorpho.

"That's right," says Batman.

As Aquaman laughs and slaps his teammates on the back, Wonder Woman is sure of it now. Batman is smiling.

The End

To follow another path, turn to page 12.

The rest of the villains in the auction hall don't move. They're shocked by the fighting between Two-Face, Black Manta, and Star Sapphire. Most of them know better than to interrupt one of Luthor's events with a pointless brawl. But some seem to be enjoying the chaos.

"Rock 'em and sock 'em, robot!" the Joker calls to Black Manta before breaking into laughter.

He's quickly slapped in the back of the head by his sometime-girlfriend, Harley Quinn. She seems to be firmly on team Star Sapphire.

Meanwhile, Batman lunges at Wonder Woman. Even his attacks perfectly copy Two-Face's moves. The strike looks real, but Wonder Woman knows it's all part of the act. She aims a pretend punch at her teammate.

Batman ducks, and Wonder Woman's fist hits Metamorpho's tank instead. Just as planned.

KKKKSSSSHHHHHHH

Greenish liquid pours onto the stage.

Batman leaps into the crowd and punches the monstrous Solomon Grundy in the stomach. Furious, Grundy lashes out.

But the Dark Knight dodges the fist. It lands right in the face of Mr. Freeze. The blow smashes the villain's protective helmet. Before he passes out from the heat, Mr. Freeze shoots a blast of super-cooled ice. It hits Gorilla Grodd and instantly freezes the great ape.

Still dressed in his Two-Face costume, Batman continues to attack random super-villains. Meanwhile on the stage, Wonder Woman throws Aquaman into the crowd. The disguised hero tumbles into Captain Cold and Mirror Master. Cheetah leaps out of their way. She smashes into Trickster. He swings wildly as he falls, trying to hit his attacker. He strikes the Joker instead.

On the stage, Metamorpho stumbles from the shattered tank. He looks out at the crowd of brawling crooks.

"Huh," he mutters. "Do I even want to know what's going on?"

Turn the page.

Wonder Woman steps near him. Metamorpho changes his fist to a large, iron mace and gets ready to fight Star Sapphire.

"It's me," she whispers.

"Wonder Woman?" Metamorpho asks. "What is all this?"

"Let's just say our distraction worked, and keep it at that," Wonder Woman replies.

She grabs Metamorpho and flies out of the room. Batman and Aquaman soon follow behind. The three meet on a nearby rooftop.

"The rest of the League should be here in two minutes to wrap things up," says Batman. "If anyone inside is still conscious by then. In the meantime, I suggest changing back to our uniforms to avoid any further confusion."

Aquaman and Wonder Woman would do just that—if they hadn't already begun to shed their super-villain costumes the second they landed on the roof.

The End

To follow another path, turn to page 12.

With all his strength, Aquaman punches Metamorpho's tank. He has to make up for what he did. He has to free his teammate.

Wonder Woman looks over at the mass of powerful super-villains climbing onto the stage. She pulls at Aquaman's arm again.

"We don't have time," Wonder Woman warns.

The Sea King tugs away from her grip. "We'll make time," he responds.

He punches the tank again. A small crack forms in its center.

Wonder Woman sighs. Then she and Aquaman both strike the tank at the same time.

FWWWWOOOOOOOSSSSSSHHHH

Aquaman steps back as water gushes out of the tank and across the stage. The small flood sweeps a few villains off their feet.

Unfortunately, most of the criminals are ready for this fight. The crowd lunges at the heroes.

Turn to page 87.

Aquaman punches an attacking villain—the Superman enemy Metallo. As the metal menace falls to the ground, Aquaman glances back at the tank. Somehow, Metamorpho is gone!

Wonder Woman looks over at Aquaman, and then she spots the empty tank too. All the while, she dodges attacks from her ferocious enemy, Cheetah.

"Where is Metamorpho?" Aquaman yells.

He grabs Metallo and flings him into the massive villain Gorilla Grodd. Both crooks are knocked out cold.

"We'll figure that out later," says Wonder Woman. "We need to get out of here. NOW!"

Wonder Woman ducks beneath Cheetah's swiping claws. She crouches down. Then she shoots off into the air and straight through the ceiling.

KRABOOOM!!!

Turn to page 95.

The emergency lights aboard the ship begin to flicker. Batman needs to get out of there, before the ship crashes. Wonder Woman can break in and grab Metamorpho later. After all, she's near-invulnerable. He's not.

Mongul watches as the light flashes from red to darkness, red to darkness. During one of the flickers, Mongul is looking at Two-Face. During the next, Batman stands in his place.

"Very dramatic," Mongul says.

THUNK!

The ship lurches again. Wonder Woman must still be outside and punching at full strength.

Batman doesn't waste any more time. He races to the large bay door. He needs to find a way to open it in order to leave the ship.

But as the Dark Knight investigates, Mongul sees his own chance to escape. He rushes to the hallway door. He leaves the chamber with Metamorpho's tank still under his arm.

Just like that, Batman's plans have changed again.

The heavy bay door won't budge. And Batman realizes Mongul must be headed to the ship's controls. If the villain gets it flying straight, he could blast away from Earth. Wonder Woman won't be able to help either Batman or Metamorpho then.

The hero runs after Mongul. But he's too late. The door to the hall slams shut. The Dark Knight immediately turns to the control panel by the doorway. Then he gets to work.

* * *

Meanwhile, Mongul stumbles toward the cockpit. He pushes his guards aside as he enters.

"Out of the way, you idiots!" he shouts.

Mongul sets the large tank down next to one of the command chairs. Taking a seat behind a set of controls, he presses a series of buttons.

The spaceship's engines begin to hum louder.

Turn the page.

FZZZZOOOOOOOOMMMM!

Even Mongul finds the need to grip the command chair as his spaceship zooms forward at full speed. It bursts out of Earth's atmosphere and into deep space. The extreme force causes Metamorpho's tank to slide. It hits a wall in the cockpit and shatters.

"Urrrgh," Metamorpho says as he falls onto the floor and opens his eyes.

When Metamorpho finally regains his focus, he's not sure he's happy to be awake. The face of Mongul stares down at him.

"The worst of your journey is now over," says Mongul. "We have come to my planet. Here, you will fight in my gladiatorial games. We have arrived at Warworld."

"Don't worry, Metamorpho," says Batman's voice from the doorway. "We won't be staying long."

Turn to page 100.

"Two-Face," says Lex Luthor from behind the podium on the stage. "Your bid still stands at one hundred million. Do I hear . . . two?"

"This isn't going to work," Wonder Woman whispers to Batman.

While his expression as Two-Face doesn't change, Batman knows his teammate is correct. The chaos from Darkseid's sudden arrival and exit has everyone in the room on edge. Their chance of rescuing Metamorpho without backup has grown increasingly slim.

The villains are watching "Two-Face." They're inspecting his every move. They're sure to notice soon that something isn't right.

"Two hundred million," Gorilla Grodd calls. The criminals all look toward his booming voice.

Batman is grateful for the distraction.

"Let's go," he whispers to his teammates.

Turn the page.

Batman, Wonder Woman, and Aquaman begin to work their way out of the auction hall. They try to slip away quietly, but Lex Luthor notices them pushing through the crowd.

"You're giving up already?" Luthor says. "Not even a pair of bids? That's unlike you, Two-Face."

Batman stops. He can feel Wonder Woman and Aquaman tense up beside him. He turns toward the podium.

In his best Two-Face voice the Dark Knight says, "This is getting *too* rich for my blood."

Luthor smirks. "Very well."

The trio starts toward the exit again.

"Three hundred million!" the Joker suddenly shouts. "Or better yet, make that four hundred if you throw in Batsy over there."

Batman's eyes widen. He shouldn't be surprised that the Joker has seen through his disguise. But he is surprised, just the same.

Turn to page 94.

On the stage, Luthor frowns. "Is that right, Joker?" he asks. "Is that Batman under all that Two-Face makeup?"

"If it's not, then I'm not wearing panty hose under this suit," the Joker says. His grin widens.

"I'm just going to take your word on both accounts," replies Luthor.

Batman looks at the crowd. The super-villains are all staring back at him. They don't seem happy about this new development. Some crack their knuckles. Others ready their weapons.

"You're really going to believe the Joker over—" Wonder Woman begins.

ZAAAAAAAPPPP!

But she's interrupted. Aquaman fires a laser eye blast from Black Manta's helmet into the mass of criminals.

Turn to page 103.

"Huh," says Aquaman, looking up at the hole Wonder Woman made in the ceiling. "I guess that works."

He dodges Captain Boomerang's flying weapon and throws a punch at the criminal. Then he squats down and jumps after his teammate.

The Sea King stumbles when he lands on the roof. He realizes just how weak he's become. He's never at full strength when he's been out of his natural watery element for too long. Then Aquaman looks around the rooftop, and he knows he needs that strength more than ever.

Because Wonder Woman and Aquaman are already surrounded.

Around them stand the energy-sapping Parasite, the weather-controlling Weather Wizard, and the yellow ring-wearing Sinestro. All three villains got to the building's rooftop as quickly as the heroes.

Turn the page.

Parasite darts forward. Aquaman tries to jump out of the way, but he's too weak. He's too slow. The villain puts both hands on Aquaman's back.

"Argh!" yells the hero.

He feels what little strength he has left leak out of his body. It feeds Parasite's own powers.

"Aquaman!" Wonder Woman says.

She turns toward him. But she's suddenly struck by a giant yellow hammer created by Sinestro's power ring.

"Ugh," Wonder Woman groans as she falls to her knees.

Aquaman drops to the ground too. He can't help it. He just doesn't have anything left in the tank. He knows the Justice League safe house is just a few blocks away. But he can't even stand.

Parasite backs away and smiles.

Then the villain notices an odd, slightly green gas floating in the air around him.

Suddenly, Parasite, Sinestro, and Weather Wizard all fall down onto the rooftop. They're fast asleep.

"You up for a short walk?" says a voice.

Aquaman looks right and left. He can't see anyone who would be speaking.

Then the green knockout gas floating in the air slowly twists and turns. It forms into the shape of a man. Within seconds, Metamorpho is standing right in front of his Justice League teammate. He was freed from the tank after all!

But the Sea King shakes his head. "I—I can't even stand," he says. "I'm too weak."

Metamorpho hears shouts from the room below them. In less than a minute, they'll be surrounded by some of the world's worst super-villains.

He looks at the unconscious Wonder Woman, and then back at Aquaman. "Well, I can't carry both of ya," he says. "But I think I have a solution."

Turn the page.

Metamorpho focuses. He has the ability to turn himself into any element or combination of elements found in the human body.

Right now, he chooses an easy one. He changes to water. Two parts hydrogen and one part oxygen.

Aquaman feels the water splash down onto his shoulders. It floods over his skin. Just like that, the Sea King gets a burst of strength. He's not at full power, but he's better.

Aquaman jumps to his feet as Metamorpho turns back to his human form. The elemental hero lifts Wonder Woman into his arms.

"Oof," says Metamorpho. "She's heavier than she looks."

Aquaman smiles. "Pure muscle is like that."

The shouts and yells from the auction hall suddenly get louder. The rest of the villains must be making their way to the roof.

"Sounds like it's time to move," Metamorpho says. He and Aquaman leap off the rooftop.

Soon Metamorpho and Aquaman reach the nearby Justice League safe house. Luckily, no one followed them. The villains are still busy searching the rooftops near the auction house.

By the time they get inside, Wonder Woman is already awake and back to her old self. She turns on the computer system.

"Wonder Woman to Justice League," she says. "We have an emergency in Gotham City. Batman has been captured. Repeat, Batman has been captured."

Wonder Woman sends out the coordinates of the auction house and then turns to look at her teammates. "Rested?" she asks.

"Never," says Aquaman.

"Good to go?" she asks.

"Always," says Aquaman.

Without another word, the three heroes rush back into the night to face the danger head-on.

The End

To follow another path, turn to page 12.

"Your League isn't here, Batman," says Mongul. On the floor, Metamorpho tries to stand. But he's too weak. "We are light-years from Earth. This is my domain."

Batman doesn't answer. Instead he throws a Batarang. Mongul dodges the attack.

The weapon wedges into the control panel. The Batarang starts to beep. Mongul's eyes widen.

KABOOOOOMMMM!!!

The Batarang explodes. It sends Mongul flying across the cockpit. Batman dives forward and slides next to Metamorpho.

"Blast shield," Batman manages to say to his teammate. Then the force of the explosion knocks him out.

Metamorpho uses the last of his strength to transform into a steel pod that closes around Batman. He fills the inside of the blast shield with a mix of fire-resistant foam and oxygen.

As Mongul's ship erupts into flames, Metamorpho is flung into space.

Turn to page 102.

A few minutes later, Batman wakes up. "Situation?" he asks.

He switches on a small flashlight from his Utility Belt. All around him is the steel of Metamorpho's protective pod.

"Best I can figure, we're in orbit around Warworld," Metamorpho says. "Looks like Mongul and his people made it to their planet."

Batman pushes a button on his belt. It sends out an emergency signal. He knows Metamorpho is too weak to get them to Warworld. He also knows his own oxygen is limited. Their only hope is that a Justice League member is nearby to notice the signal. Maybe someone can come to the rescue.

"This isn't good, is it, Bats?" asks Metamorpho.

But Batman doesn't answer. He needs to save his oxygen. And he doesn't have anything to say, anyway.

The End

To follow another path, turn to page 12.

"The jig is up, Diana," Aquaman says from under his Black Manta costume. He punches the Riddler as he speaks. "No use in pretending any longer!"

The Riddler falls to the floor. But the dozens of super-villains standing behind him don't look like they'll go down as easily.

"We really need to work on your subtlety," Wonder Woman tells Aquaman as more fierce foes charge toward them.

Wonder Woman grabs her enemy, Cheetah, and hurls her into the massive Gorilla Grodd. They tumble back into four other criminals.

"There's only one thing we need to work on right now," says Batman as he sweeps the legs out from underneath Harley Quinn. "And that's an exit strategy."

Suddenly, a boxing glove flies across the room and smacks into Batman's chest.

KABOOOOOM!

Turn the page.

Seconds later, the Joker stands over the unconscious Dark Knight. The Clown Prince of Crime is holding a gun with a comically large barrel. It's still smoking.

"If you want something done right," says the Joker, "you're better off packing an exploding boxing-glove cannon in your pants."

"I don't think that's the saying, puddin'," says Harley Quinn as she walks up to her boyfriend.

Wonder Woman and Aquaman can't come to their friend's rescue. They're too busy with their own battles.

The Sea King dodges the icy blasts of both Mr. Freeze and Captain Cold. Wonder Woman is slugging it out with the massive Giganta and Solomon Grundy.

But more and more villains join in the fight. In less than a minute, both Aquaman and Wonder Woman are on the ground. They're as unconscious as Batman.

"We're going to stop messing around," Lex Luthor says from the podium a short while later. "The bidding starts at one billion dollars."

No one argues. They know that the price is worth it. The winning bidder still gets the hero Metamorpho to use as the "ultimate weapon." But now he or she will also get Batman, Wonder Woman, and Aquaman in the deal. The starting bid is quite a bargain, all things considered.

"One billion!" shouts Sinestro, the Yellow Lantern.

"Two!" yells Gorilla Grodd.

"Four billion," calls the Joker. The criminals all turn and stare. "What? I'm good for it."

On the stage stand four tanks. Each Justice League member floats helplessly in one of the green-tinted containers. And outside, the super-villains laugh.

The End

To follow another path, turn to page 12.

AUTHOR

The author of the Amazon best-selling hardcover *Batman: A Visual History*, Matthew K. Manning has contributed to many comic books, including *Beware the Batman*, *Spider-Man Unlimited*, *Batman/Teenage Mutant Ninja Turtles Adventures*, *Justice League Adventures*, *Looney Tunes*, and *Scooby Doo, Where Are You?* When not writing comics themselves, Manning often authors books about them, as well as a series of young reader books starring Superman, Batman, and The Flash for Capstone. He currently lives in Asheville, North Carolina, with his wife, Dorothy, and their two daughters, Lillian and Gwendolyn. Visit him online at www.matthewkmanning.com.

ILLUSTRATOR

Erik Doescher is a concept artist for Gearbox Software and a professional illustrator. He attended the School of Visual Arts in New York City and has freelanced for DC Comics for almost twenty years, in addition to many other licensed properties. He lives in Texas with his wife, five kids, two cats, and two fish.

GLOSSARY

auction (AWK-shuhn)—a sale during which items are sold to the person who offers the most money

canopy (KA-nuh-pee)—the sliding cover found over a vehicle's or aircraft's main controls

cloaking (CLOH-king)—the ability to hide from sight

dummy (DUH-mee)—a copy that's made to look like the real thing and be used in its place; also, a stupid person

element (EL-uh-muhnt)—a substance that cannot be broken down into simpler substances; all matter is made of elements

gladiator (GLAD-ee-ay-ter)—a person who is forced to fight for the entertainment of others

grapnel (GRAP-nuhl)—a device with metal claws attached to the end of a cord, used to drag or hook onto something

hangar (HANG-ur)—an area where aircraft are parked

hologram (HOL-uh-gram)—a 3D image made using light

invulnerable (in-VUHL-ner-uh-buhl)—impossible to injure

safe house (SAYF HOUSS)—a secret hiding place for members of a group

teleport (TEL-uh-pawrt)—to move from one place to another instantly

tyrant (TYE-ruhnt)—a leader who rules other people in a cruel or unjust way

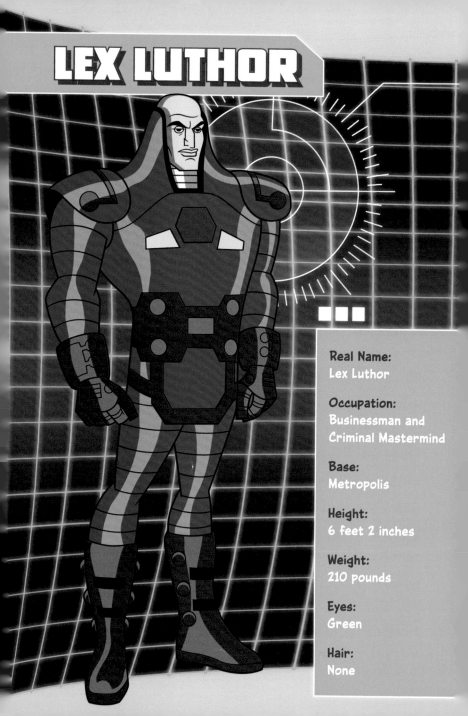

LEX LUTHOR

Real Name:
Lex Luthor

Occupation:
Businessman and
Criminal Mastermind

Base:
Metropolis

Height:
6 feet 2 inches

Weight:
210 pounds

Eyes:
Green

Hair:
None

Lex Luthor is one of the richest and most powerful people in the city of Metropolis. To many people he's known as a successful businessman, but Luthor has a dirty secret— most of his wealth is ill-gotten, and behind the scenes he is a criminal mastermind. Superman has stopped many of Luthor's sinister schemes. But the villain is careful to never get caught red-handed, so he's free to plan his next crime. Luthor's ultimate goal is to defeat Superman. Only then can Metropolis truly be under his total control.

- Lex Luthor is a crafty businessman, but he's also a criminal mastermind. He often recruits other super-villains to help carry out his illegal activities and to try to topple Superman—and anyone else who would dare stand in his way.

- Luthor has no superpowers, but he is a genius. He uses his superior smarts to make incredible inventions. These include his trademark armored battle suit, which gives him powers and abilities similar to the Man of Steel's.

- In an attempt to become even more powerful, Luthor once schemed his way into the office of President of the United States! It ended badly for him, however, when people discovered that he had secretly put the world at risk to increase his approval ratings.

STRENGTH IN NUMBERS

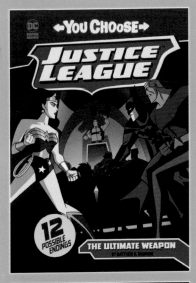